TEAM SPIRIT!™

# MARCHING BAND

Frank Coachman

rosen central™

The Rosen Publishing Group, Inc., New York

Published in 2007 by The Rosen Publishing Group, Inc.
29 East 21st Street, New York, NY 10010

First Edition

**Library of Congress Cataloging-in-Publication Data**

Coachman, Frank.
Marching band / by Frank Coachman.
   p. cm.—(Team spirit!)
Includes bibliographical references and index.
ISBN 1-4042-0730-9 (library binding)
1. Marching bands.
I. Title. II. Team spirit! (New York, N.Y.)
MT733.C59 2007
784.8'3—dc22

2006003788

*Manufactured in the United States of America*

**On the cover:** The Michigan State University Spartan Band bass drum line entertains the crowd at a football game in September 2005.

# CONTENTS

# A Beautiful Noise

Trumpets blare, cymbals clash, and drums rattle and boom, shaking the seats in the stadium as if to jolt already excited football fans into frenzied celebration. In an instant, the home crowd chants along to the tune played by its school's marching band. The fans are cheering themselves as much as the athletes they have come to support. As the horn blasts subside, the action on the field resumes. At the end of the play, the band from the visiting school—accompanied by its own throng of roaring fans—fills the stadium with its proud noise. Such are the festivities at high school football games.

Saxophone and sousaphone players of the Etiwanda High School marching band from Etiwanda, California, execute a left march column during a Bands of America regional championship in Long Beach, California, in October 2005.

Although it's easy to spot in the stands during the game, it is at halftime that the full majesty of the marching band is showcased. From the high-strutting drum major leading the band on the field to the baton-twirling majorettes and tumbling pom squad to the color guard with its dazzling flag displays to the musicians who march in rhythmic strides as they maneuver themselves into impressive formations, each marching band—often hundreds of members strong—puts on a spectacular show.

Judging from the boisterous response, it is clear that the spectators at football games come not only to watch an exciting game. They also expect to be a part of the revelry surrounding the game. The marching band plays a major role in making this happen by creating excitement through music. As such, it is a catalyst of spirit for a school or community.

In many ways, the marching band is the anchor of the American pageantry movement, which includes cheerleading, dance teams, indoor percussion ensembles, drum corps, and winter guards. It is the oldest of the pageantry activities, and many of the other activities emerged from the marching band tradition. Within the ranks of modern marching bands—some of which have more than 500 members—are nonmusical auxiliary groups, such as pom squads, drill teams, twirlers, and color guards. These represent pageantry activities in their own right.

Beyond the football field, marching bands are very much part of the fabric of American life. For more than a century, they have provided

University bands contribute to the overall spirit and enthusiasm of the crowd during football games. This band is performing the school fight song after its team has scored a touchdown.

the soundtrack to many of the nation's special events, including presidential inaugurations and parades commemorating historic anniversaries and civic pride. As such, the marching band has become the icon of American pomp and circumstance.

# CHAPTER 1

# The Evolution of Marching Band

**A** marching band is a musical ensemble that performs mainly outdoors and incorporates movement into its performances. Within the American pageantry tradition, these bands are usually associated with educational institutions, where they play a significant role in boosting school spirit, usually at sporting events. They also represent the schools in marching band competitions.

The bass drummer pays close attention to the drum major in order to be completely in synchronization with the rest of the band.

## A Military Tradition

Today's marching band has its roots in the military tradition of using musical units to help move troops in an orderly and expedient fashion over great distances. For several centuries, the instrumentation of the military band remained the same: the fife and drum were associated with the infantry, while the trumpet and kettledrum were associated with the cavalry. France introduced the oboe in the latter half of the seventeenth century, and over the following decades other instruments were added to the army bands of the world's most powerful countries.

During the American Revolutionary War period, the infantry used drums to establish a pulse to march thousands of troops from one location to another. It used fifes to play melodies to heighten the spirits of the troops. The cavalry used bugles and kettledrums to issue

This photograph shows members of the 48th Regiment band of the New York Volunteer Infantry at Fort Pulaski, Georgia, around 1863 during the Civil War.

orders and commands to distant riders. During the American Civil War, field marching bands were typically composed of civilians who played drums and bugles.

In the 1800s, the need for marching bands to assist in moving troops diminished, and the concert band movement took hold in the United States. After the Civil War, Congress passed a bill authorizing the creation of concert bands within the structure of the military. These bands marched primarily for military ceremonies and for street parades.

John Philip Sousa, known as the March King, is one of the United States' most famous composers. He invented the sousaphone and wrote "The Stars and Stripes Forever," which is the official march of the United States.

In 1880, John Philip Sousa was appointed director of the Marine Band, which he developed as a civilian concert band. The primary role of the Marine Band was to provide entertainment. Like the other military concert bands, it performed mainly the music composed by its director. According to Encarta Online Encyclopedia, Sousa, a perfectionist, "raised the level of performance and instrumentation of the concert band. He composed so many marches, he is known as the March King."

Sousa's marches were well suited for street marching. Soon, there were numerous other composers creating music in the march style. Among them, the most popular were Kenneth Alford, C. L. Barnhouse, Henry Fillmore, Karl L. King, and Roland Seitz.

## College Bands

The popularity of these military musicians spurred a marching band movement among American colleges. By the beginning of the twentieth century, college bands began to provide halftime entertainment at football games. The groups customarily performed in marching block designs—in which the musicians are positioned in ranks (rows) and files (columns)—and played traditional march music. As the years passed, college bands seeking to distinguish themselves experimented with both marching styles and music selection. As a result, several styles of marching on the football field have evolved. Of these, the show band style, which has many variations, is the most common. It uses popular music arranged for marching band instrumentation. Moreover, bands added auxiliary units, such as color guards and majorettes, to add visual flair to their performances.

By the middle of the twentieth century, marching bands were common in high schools. These high school bands generally followed the trends set at the college level. However, high school bands have tried their own innovative ways to present their shows, especially in light of the many marching band competitions that have emerged since the 1970s.

## Elements of a Marching Band

Marching bands vary widely in size, ranging from fewer than 20 members to more than 500. Accordingly, the structure and instrumentation

Large marching bands generally include playing and nonplaying members, as well as marching and nonmarching members. The young ladies dancing with the mock rifles are part of the color guard. The sideline percussion section in the forefront presents a tremendous addition to the general effect of the music.

of the modern marching band is very flexible. Some bands include only musicians. However, most high school and college marching bands have a section of nonplaying members who add a visual flair to the bands' presentation. This section is known as the band front, or auxiliary. It typically consists of a color guard and at least one drum major, but it also often includes majorettes and a pom squad.

# Classification of Musical Instruments

Generally, musical instruments are grouped into categories called families according to the way they produce sounds. Traditionally, there are four main families: strings, woodwinds, brass, and percussion. The sounds of string instruments result from the vibration of their strings, which may be plucked or played with a bow. A woodwind produces sounds by the vibration of its reed (or reeds) when the player blows air into it. A brass instrument makes sounds when the player's lips vibrate against the mouthpiece as he or she blows air into its column. Percussion instruments produce sounds when they are struck, shaken, scraped, rubbed, or scratched.

Some instruments are not easily classified. The piano, for example, has strings that vibrate when struck by its hammers. As such, it may be classified as either a string or a percussion instrument. Moreover, there are alternative ways of classifying instruments. Some musicians classify all instruments that are played with a keyboard into a separate category. The human voice is considered to be the first instrument.

Of course, musicians form the core of the marching band. They are usually grouped according to the type of instruments they play. The standard instrumentation of the modern marching band includes brass, woodwind, and percussion instruments. Among the brass instruments,

The flute section of the Tiger Marching Band is tuning and warming up prior to its performance in a competition.

trumpets, horns, trombones, baritones, cornets, and tubas are most common. The woodwind section typically includes piccolos, flutes, clarinets, and saxophones. Snares, clash cymbals, and bass and tenor drums of various sizes are the usual percussion instruments.

Many marching bands include percussionists who do not march because their instruments are too large and unwieldy to be carried around the field. This subsection of the percussion group is called the pit, or sideline. It may include bells, a xylophone, a marimba, chimes, and timpani. Though uncommon, some marching bands include stringed instruments, such as guitars, as well as electronic instruments, usually in the pit.

In 1975, Gene Smith, director of instrumental music at Cameron University in Lawton, Oklahoma, said, "It cannot be overlooked that the marching band or, to be more specific, the football marching band, is a unique phenomenon found only in the United States, and largely parallels the degree to which the quality and quantity of school band programs have developed during the past fifty years." Since then, the marching band has evolved beyond its roots in support of sports teams and parades. Today's marching band performs spectacular stage shows with elaborate props, staging, dancing, and acrobatics.

# CHAPTER 2

# Skills Needed for Marching Band

Consider the words "marching" and "band." "Marching" can be described as moving along steadily, usually with a rhythmic stride and in step with others. It may also be defined as moving in a direct and purposeful manner. A member of a marching unit must possess the rhythmic skill and physical control to move in time to a beat

This student is playing a tenor saxophone. In addition to playing the instrument well, he is expected to make sure that he is always in the right place at the right time during the marching band's performance.

or pulse and coordinate this movement in perfect unison with other members of the band. The performer's feet must move in synchronization, or in time, with the music. In essence, the marching members of the band should be able to stand for long periods of time; control movement of body parts in rhythmic synchronization; read and understand map coordinates; play an instrument; and memorize sequences, patterns, locations in a formation, and movements.

The word "band" in this context refers to a group of musicians organized for ensemble playing and chiefly using woodwind, brass, and percussion instruments. In order to be a successful member of a

The snare drum section practices its featured section of the show prior to a performance. Not only must the drumming be performed perfectly together, but the visual presentation of arm motion, wrist action, and stick movements must also be unified.

marching band, one must develop musical skills and become proficient with a musical instrument. In most schools, the process of learning to play a musical instrument usually begins in the fifth or sixth grade. Traditionally, the first few years of learning do not involve marching, but focus mainly on developing the skills necessary to perform proficiently on an instrument of the student's choice.

# Marching Styles

There are two main marching styles: The traditional parade style, or marching block design; and the show band style, which has several variations. The marching block design is demonstrated keenly today by the Texas A&M University Aggie Band. The stride from one step to another is 30 inches (76 centimeters), or 6 steps to 5 yards (4.6 meters). This is commonly called "6-to-5." The band moves in company fronts (rows) and files, which can create the shapes of blocks and diagonals. Changes to the formations are created through the use of left and right turns, to-the-rears (180-degree change of direction), and countermarches.

The show band style, which uses popular music arranged for marching band instrumentation, is mainly straight lines that are manipulated into diagonals, pinwheels, and occasional arcs and circles. University bands that premiered this style and still utilize it today are those of the University of Michigan, Texas Tech University, and the University of Texas. The stride is 22½ inches (57 cm), or 8 steps to 5 yards (4.6 m). It is referred to as "8-to-5." This style evolved further into more curvilinear designs that use multiple strides or differing strides for each performer when transitioning from one formation to another. It has been commonly called "corps style," because of roots in the drum and bugle corps competition format begun in the 1970s.

Seated in a concert band setting, these instrumentalists rehearse basic fundamentals needed to ensure their success when performing music.

## Beginning Bands

Making the decision to become an instrumentalist can be very exciting for the beginning musician. School music teachers provide opportunities for the student to investigate various instruments and assistance in making the correct choice to ensure the student's success. Most instruments in a concert band, which typically does not involve movement, are also used in the marching band. There are a few exceptions: the double reed woodwinds, which include the oboe, the bassoon, the English horn, and the contrabassoon.

Beginning band programs do not offer all of the marching band instruments during the first year or two of training. The beginning classes usually focus on the basic members of each family of instruments. Beginning woodwind classes usually include instruction on flute, clarinet, and alto saxophone. Beginning brass players will start on cornets, trumpets, trombones, baritones, and sometimes French horns and tubas. Percussionists start by learning snare drums and bells.

In most cases, the beginning student and his or her family will have to rent or purchase an instrument. Rental purchase involves monthly payments for one or two years, but the customer has the option to return the instrument at any time or keep it after the rental period is over. The instrument may also be traded in for a model closer in quality to a professional one. A beginner book is usually provided with the instrument. Some beginner books have related Web sites providing accompaniment and assessment tools that can be used with the book. This technology can be taken advantage of at home as well as at school.

All beginners are taught to expand on their prior musical knowledge, typically learned in music classes in the first through fourth or fifth grades. Each instrument has its own unique attributes and challenges to explore and master. Students must learn the proper manner in which to sit and hold the instrument, the right breathing technique for wind instruments, and the correct embouchure (the manner in which

Through sharing the joy of learning music, these young students could ultimately become friends for life.

the lips and tongue are applied to the mouthpiece or reed of a wind instrument). Percussionists must learn proper techniques for holding sticks and mallets. All students learn to properly care for their instruments and accessories.

The first few years of playing an instrument involve learning to read music and its two main dimensions of rhythm and melody, then equating these skills to the performance of the instrument. The work is challenging, but the reward for achieving musical success is very satisfying.

Learning to carry the cymbals in like fashion is an important first step for these marching percussion students.

As beginners progress individually, their ability to play in synchronization with others makes the class a true band. The band will explore many types of music, including pop tunes, folk songs, traditional marches, and classical selections. The exploration of this music affords each student the chance to attain the skills necessary to audition for the marching band. Starting the process in the beginning band program and continuing to learn to become proficient on an instrument through the middle school years provide the best avenue for success.

Many middle school band programs do not include marching bands. Nevertheless, spirit bands that perform at the school's athletic events provide valuable training for high school marching bands. Spirit bands probably do not march at these events, but the music is very similar to what is performed by marching bands. Spirit bands also perform concerts and may participate in competitive events. All of these activities further prepare the music student for a successful audition with the high school band.

## Band Camp

Many college and university music programs offer band camps during summer vacation. Most are usually age- or grade-level specific and can last from four to ten days. These camps are excellent opportunities for students to study privately, in pairs, or in small groups with professionals. They also provide an environment many students may not have access to through their school programs. Besides playing in one of the camp bands, students can elect to take classes in music theory, conducting, and drum majoring and leadership. Most camps offer great recreational opportunities as well.

# CHAPTER 3

# Becoming and Being a Marching Band Member

**S**ometime during the spring semester, high school band programs begin recruiting and holding auditions for their marching bands. Each program has a unique method of conducting this event. Usually there is a music performance audition consisting of a prepared piece of music, a performance of scales, and possibly an etude (study exercise) or excerpt to be sight-read. (Sight-reading is the reading

The baritone saxophone is the largest of the woodwind instruments and requires strong physical stamina of the performer.

and performing of a piece of music from a score without having seen it before.) It is important to watch the calendar for an audition, obtain the required documents and audition materials, and register or submit any required paperwork before the deadline. Begin preparing early. Many high school bands use a Web site to conduct most of this process.

## The Audition

The audition may be conducted at the student's current school, or it may require a visit to the high school facility. In most cases the audition is live, but a few programs use a recording process. In all cases, the director of the

A trombone player enjoys the benefits of a private lesson from a professional teacher. Private lessons afford a student the opportunity to improve specific needs.

high school program wants to hear each student perform at his or her best. It is important not to let the change from middle school to high school and fear of the unknown dissuade you from continuing to pursue your musical goals. Too often, students are intimidated by the changes they face and allow their fears to shake their confidence.

Some marching band programs conduct a marching component during the audition process. At a minicamp, for example, marching fundamentals may be demonstrated and taught by the directors or student leaders to the prospective members. The conclusion of the minicamp could be an assessment of the skills learned by the prospective member during the event. These minicamps are usually held during the beginning of summer vacation or a few weeks prior to the beginning of classes.

Most programs have a week or two of rehearsals before the start of the new school year. This intense period of rehearsal affords the members of the band a chance to develop close ties with one another, build their fundamental marching skills, improve their playing abilities, and begin learning the difficult drill patterns for field shows. These sessions include all of the members of the band. Students who are absent from these rehearsals are usually not considered for performance opportunities.

During summer band, a series of rehearsals held during summer vacation, you can expect extended practice periods of several hours during the day. There might even be an evening session along with the day rehearsal two or three times a week. Since the traditional school year begins in August or September, the weather can be quite warm, especially in the Southern states. Students can expect to be uncomfortable at times and should be prepared to deal with the heat. Frequent breaks and hydration are essential in maintaining proper health and avoiding heatstroke.

## Mentors

New marching band members can also expect to be assigned some type of leader or mentor to assist them with learning the traditions and operations of the program. This person may be a simple "band buddy," "big brother," "big sister," or a section leader or captain. These are experienced band members who have earned the right to serve as squad or team leaders. They facilitate the teaching and assessment of performances. Squads and teams are most often composed of members who play the same instrument.

The Ayala High School marching band of Chino Hills, California, practices its competition routine on the school's football field. It takes months of hard work to combine the activities of the band's various sections into one seamless show.

During marching band rehearsals, the mentors assist the members of their team with warm-up exercises, perfecting marching fundamentals, drill placements, and drill maneuvering. Performance drills for football halftime shows are often provided in map coordinate language and may include charts of a football field with letters or numbers representing each performer. Each band member finds his or her position in a given set (or formation) that makes a shape in the field, finds the next set, and then sequences the two sets together with a prescribed number of steps. These steps are referred to as the transition from one set to another. Transitions create the interesting movements within the marching component of the show. At times, there may be head, hand, arm, and upper-body choreography added to the standard foot movements to enhance the general effect of the presentation.

## Rehearsals

A typical outside marching band rehearsal begins with the squads of performers working on marching fundamentals. This period warms up the performer's body and also improves movement coordination and control. Upon completion of the physical warm-ups, the section leaders begin the music warm-ups. These include long tones and scales. The performers are seeking to perfectly match pitch and balance, blend their sound with their neighbors, and improve tone quality.

The full group assembles after the section warm-ups. They begin by playing similar long tones and chorales (hymn-like compositions, usually arranged in four parts) to establish pitch and improve the full band's tonal quality. The band is now ready to begin learning new drills, rehearsing previously learned drills, and improving the overall presentation of what they have learned. This process can be tedious, as each performer is responsible for his or her position within a drill, and these positions must be learned and memorized. Each performer must learn

Body movements add visual interest during a performance. These band members are rehearsing a leg lift during a marching band practice.

the path and step size to perfect the movement during the transition. While marching, each member must maintain his or her dress, cover, interval, and distance. Dress is the alignment with a person to a side; cover is the alignment with a person to the front; interval is the spacing between persons on either side; and distance is the space between persons in front and behind.

A marching drill can be learned and cleaned to recorded music, with the actual tempos reduced. The live music is added to the drill when the footwork and positioning on the field are second nature to all of the band members. The performance of the music and the movement of all of the performers must be done in complete synchronization, giving the impression that the band is one large entity. Phasing of sound can occur when one side of the band differs from the other in exact timing of the music. Because of the wide arrangement of performers on a football field, the sound will lag (phase) from one end to the other. The performers must all produce the music at precisely the same instant or phasing will occur. It is this perfection of sound and movement, along with the band's ability to create an effective musical performance, that is judged at competitions. It is sometimes necessary to be repetitive to the point of tedium so that all members of the band will achieve the desired level of performance memory. This aspect can be trying at times, but knowing that the performance will be improved makes it worth the effort.

During the school year, school marching bands rehearse in many different schedule formats. Most school bands with marching programs rehearse the marching component of the show outside the normal school day, just as football, baseball, tennis, and basketball teams do. These rehearsals can be before or after school. Most marching band students have a music class during the school day, and this period is used to teach fundamental playing skills and to rehearse music selections.

Indoor marching band rehearsals during the school day typically consist of music warm-ups of long tones, scales, chorales, technical exercises,

Marching band shows present a series of formations. Each member is responsible for his or her position as the band transitions from one formation to the next.

and tuning. Rehearsal of the music includes the full ensemble playing together. It also includes remediation of certain sections within the band. Most marching bands require the memorization of the music to be used during performances. This process may include an individual assessment process to ensure that each member is accomplishing the memorization goals set by the directors. The entire band's level of success rests on the abilities of all performers. Each member must learn, memorize, and perform to his or her best ability.

> Being a member of the band is for everyone. Anyone can learn to contribute to the success of a musical organization.

## The Benefits of Marching Band

The time allotted to marching band in high school consists of enrolling in the school's band program, attending the regularly scheduled band class during the school day, and making the commitment to the rehearsals, meetings of leadership groups, self-practice, performances, and competitions. During the peak fall season, there may be as many as eight hours of before- or after-school practice during the school week, eight to twelve Friday-night performances, and several weekends with Saturday competitions. Although it is a major commitment, the time spent in marching band provides many opportunities to make friends. Participating in the marching band will provide many trips, social activities, hours of community service, and performances.

Membership in a marching band enhances the high school experience. Members learn about citizenship, commitment, team-building, goal setting, and leadership. The most important benefit is learning and possessing a lifelong skill of music performance. You might even have a career in music as a result of the experience.

## Leadership

Leadership responsibilities in the band come with time and experience. There are many opportunities to serve a marching band. Bands may use a military-style ranking system for the assignment of its officers, who are commonly called rank leaders. Students earn points based on their musical skills and accomplishments during each school year. These points are cumulative from year to year and are used to select the leaders within the band. A band might utilize one head drum major and two field drum majors. The head drum major is responsible for conducting the band during its field performances. The field drum majors assist the head drum major by mirror conducting on the field when and where needed during the show. Along with the points accumulated, drum majors must audition for the position.

Each of the major sections of the band has a leader, who might be called a captain or colonel. There is a woodwind leader, brass leader, percussion leader, dance team leader, and color guard leader. Each of these students is responsible for leading the students of their respective section. Each major section has a lieutenant or captain of each instrument group. The woodwind section has a flute leader, a clarinet leader, and a saxophone leader. There is also a lieutenant or captain for each of the cornet/trumpet, horn, trombone, baritone, and tuba sections. The percussion section also has a leader. Sergeants or lieutenants within each section are appointed when there are more than eight or ten in a section. The use of sergeants or lieutenants is most common for the flute, clarinet, and trumpet sections. These sections traditionally have many members.

There are many other opportunities to serve a marching band organization as a leader or crew member. The band may have a student staff that handles many organizational duties. Foremost is a team of music librarians who are responsible for making sure each band member has the correct music. There may also be student leaders who assist with inventory control of instruments and equipment. The staff may also have student leaders who handle uniform and costume issues, and another team of specialists who assist in making sure the electronic communication and public address systems are in place for rehearsals and performances.

Other students may be asked to organize the loading of equipment trucks when traveling to and from performance locations. On each band bus there may be students responsible for assisting the chaperones (supervising adults) with roll call and attendance. Preparing and serving water and other refreshments during rehearsals and at football games may be another task for the student crew. If there is a need for something as simple as posting spirit signs in the band hall, there is a need for student leaders to accomplish such goals.

The many social events the band program staff chooses to offer may require the use of a council of students who assist in planning the events. The band may elect a president, vice president, secretary, and

Woodwind instruments can be damaged by wet weather. In order to optimize the rehearsal schedule, the band will practice drill formations and transitions without instruments.

treasurer, along with representatives from each of the major sections of the band, in order to have a team of student leaders to assist in planning and facilitating its social events.

## Health and Injuries

Maintaining good health helps to ensure success as a musician and a marcher. The fundamental marching warm-up routines should be taken seriously and utilized before every marching rehearsal. Playing instruments—especially wind instruments—while marching places significant stress on the body's muscles. Therefore, it is important that band members are in excellent physical condition.

There are several other precautions to take. A marcher and wind instrument performer should restrain from smoking. Smoking is unhealthy for everyone, but combining it with the demands of marching band stresses the lungs even further, especially for those who play wind instruments or carry heavier equipment like bass drums, quin-toms, and tubas.

Another health risk in this environment is drinking from the same cup or thermos used by other students. Mononucleosis is a common virus among teens and is easily spread through shared drinking sources. Avoid drinking after others and use a personal cup or thermos. Do not use another person's instrument without first disinfecting the mouthpiece. Do not share mouthpieces with others.

Using proper posture and hand position will help band members avoid skeletal and muscular injuries and carpal tunnel syndrome, a painful condition of the hand and forearm. Holding an instrument tightly may cause chronic pain if the tension is prolonged. Be sure to have your posture, hand positions, and finger positions checked regularly by other performers or directors to ensure that you are using the proper methods. This will help you avoid injury and allow the best possible environment for success. Percussionists carrying the heavier pieces should always stand by using a knee bend upward and not lift the equipment off the ground with their backs.

# CHAPTER 4

# Performances and Competitions

**A**lthough marching bands began with traditional marches, today's college and high school versions perform music in the baroque, classical, romantic, impressionist, and modern styles, along with pieces from movie soundtracks and other popular tunes.

The majority of a band's performances are done during halftime shows at the school's varsity football games. In

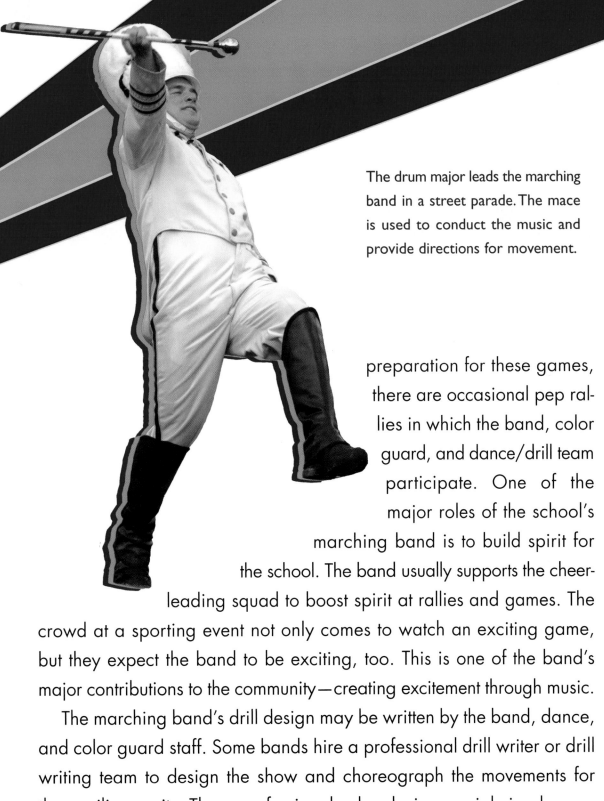

The drum major leads the marching band in a street parade. The mace is used to conduct the music and provide directions for movement.

preparation for these games, there are occasional pep rallies in which the band, color guard, and dance/drill team participate. One of the major roles of the school's marching band is to build spirit for the school. The band usually supports the cheerleading squad to boost spirit at rallies and games. The crowd at a sporting event not only comes to watch an exciting game, but they expect the band to be exciting, too. This is one of the band's major contributions to the community—creating excitement through music.

The marching band's drill design may be written by the band, dance, and color guard staff. Some bands hire a professional drill writer or drill writing team to design the show and choreograph the movements for the auxiliary units. These professionals also devise special visual movements for the musicians. The successful visual integration of the drill,

Following a marching band contest performance, it is traditional for each organization to pose for a group photo.

dance, and color guard to the music is essential in creating a performance that is entertaining and potentially award-winning. The use of the proper colors in flags and other accessories is also a major factor. A band's uniform can also add or detract from the overall effect of the presentation.

## Uniforms

For many years, marching band uniforms were made of wool and mimicked the designs of European military uniforms from the nineteenth century. Examples include the uniforms of the Revolutionary War period and even the early days of the U.S. Military Academy at West Point. The fabric was very heavy and much too warm for the summer and early fall months. During the 1970s and early 1980s, lighter hybrid and synthetic fabrics were introduced. Innovative approaches to costuming among drum and bugle corps also influenced design trends in marching band uniforms.

The uniforms became much more affordable, but they still required dry-cleaning. In the past few years, uniforms have become machine-washable. Designs have also become less militaristic and more simplistically festive. Although uniforms are made from newer, lighter fabrics, there are organizations in the hottest regions of the country that delay the use of formal uniforms until weather permits. Typically, band members dress in jeans (or even shorts) and T-shirts for hot-weather performances.

## Football

A high school marching band usually arrives at a football game about forty-five minutes before kickoff. The percussionists need time to unload their equipment, and the various crews need to unload refreshments, uniform accessories, flags, props, and any electronic equipment the band may use during the game. The band also needs time to assemble for the traditional march into the stadium.

Upon arrival in the stands, each band provides a few pep tunes to entertain the crowd and "fire up" the football team as the athletes warm up. The football teams leave the field after their warm-up. Then each team's band performs its school's alma mater (anthem or song). As each

The quad-tom section of the university marching band is featured during a time-out at a football game. Quad-toms are a group of four drums of different sizes. Each drum produces a different pitch.

football team returns to the stadium for the beginning of the game, its band plays the school's fight song. The home team's band then performs "The Star-Spangled Banner" while the crowd and football teams stand with pride.

During the game, the bands take turns performing pep tunes consisting mostly of pop music, marches, movie themes, and cheer blasters. When there are about five minutes left in the first half of the game, the bands begin to move toward the sidelines for halftime. The visiting band takes the field first, followed by the home team band. Each band usually has about twelve to fourteen minutes to present its show.

An announcer introduces the show, the leaders within the bands, and any other pertinent information. Most halftime shows include a drill presentation by the band; a percussion section feature; and a special performance by the drill team, color guard, and twirlers. In this setting, the bands' critics are parents, friends, relatives, and community members. It is a great time to shine.

## Parades

The marching band is also called upon to march in community parades. These parades can be celebrations such as presidential inaugurations, Thanksgiving, Christmas, Independence Day, or other civic pride events. The band lines up in a marching block composed of ranks and files. Typically, each band member tries to stay within his or her given rank and file, maintaining even spacing with neighboring musicians. It is usually the responsibility of the people at the end of each rank and the front of each file to be in the correct location; this allows other band members to follow them.

Band members keep a constant pace or step size while marching in a parade. This usually varies between 22 and 30 inches (56 and 76 cm) per stride. A step size of 22.5 inches is called "8-to-5" because the marcher covers 5 yards (4.6 m) in 8 steps. A step size of 30 inches is called "6-to-5" because 5 yards are covered in 6 steps. Because yard

The Charles Flowers High School band marches in a July 4th parade in Springdale, Maryland. Local parades offer great performance opportunities for high school marching bands.

lines on an American football field are 5 yards apart, 8-to-5 and 6-to-5 steps are most useful for field shows. A drum cadence is played when the band is marching but not playing a song. This is how the band keeps time. The cadence tempo varies from band to band, but it is generally between 110 and 144 beats per minute.

Parades usually offer twenty to thirty minutes of marching performance. These are great public-relations opportunities for the band. Parades such as the Macy's Thanksgiving Day Parade and the Rose Parade can last for more than two hours.

## Competitions

Most marching bands participate in field show championships. These competitions can be school-sponsored regional events leading to state-level competitions, or regional and national championships sponsored by Bands of America. These competitions are usually divided into classes based on the size of the school or the size of the band. There are usually four or five classes of competition, which are usually A, AA, AAA, AAAA, or AAAAA.

Some bands choose to participate in two or three competitions each year, while others create an entire season of six to eight competitive events. There are many bands that host such events. The hosting band usually does not compete with its guests but presents its show in exhibition only. Hosting such an event requires community resources and a lot of parental involvement.

In Texas, for instance, a high school marching band may participate in two or three marching festivals to prepare for its school-sponsored regional, area, and state contests. The school-sponsored events offer advancement from the regional-level contest to the area-level contest for any band that receives a superior rating. There are preliminary and final rounds at the area contest, and at least two bands advance to the state contest from each of the five classes. This number increases based on the number of bands that have been certified in the class from the regional event. At the state-level event, there is a preliminary stage and a finals stage. The top ten bands from the preliminaries will advance to the finals.

These two horn players are standing on ladders to enhance their visual and auditory presentation during a duet.

These preliminaries and finals are held on the same day and extend into the evening.

Rules and regulations governing marching band contests vary from state to state and from festival to festival. However, most have common concepts that must be followed. In certain states that follow a unified or school-sanctioned contest plan, there may be rules governing the start date on which a band may begin learning drill and/or music for its competitive season each year. There may also be budgetary constraints with respect to music arranging, drill designing, props, and other factors. Rules such as these are intended to level the playing field for all of the participants, creating a fair contest based on music presentation and marching execution.

At field marching band competitions, each band is allowed a standard warm-up period before the show. This can be in an indoor location, outdoor location, or a combination of the two. The band's entry onto the field of competition has a time limit, and the group is announced about

This college halftime show features four mirrored symmetrical circles with inner-to-outer circles executing contrary motion.

one minute prior to its scheduled start time. The announcement includes the group's name, directors' names, program of music, and an introduction of the band's drum majors. The final words of the announcer before the performance are, "Drum majors: is your band ready?" The drum majors perform a salute to the audience, which includes the judges and, at the announcer's prompt, signals the band to begin playing.

Typically, the length of the show is restricted to between eight and twelve minutes, depending on particular contest rules. The stadium clock may be used during this period. There may also be restrictions on the use of electronic instruments or devices on or off the field and the use or placement of props, as well as the participation of adults or directors during the performance. Following the performance, there is usually a timed exit period that may have stipulations regarding the use of sound or silence.

## Judging

Judging of the marching band contest is based on music performance, marching performance, auxiliary unit effectiveness, and the overall effect of the presentation. A judge evaluating the music performance should provide constructive criticism with respect to the brass, woodwind, and percussion sections' tone quality, intonation, balance and blend, technique, and effective use. The overall ensemble's performance is evaluated with comments concerning balance and blend, rhythmic precision, intonation, articulation, suitability of the music, phrasing, dynamics, tempos, and musical styles.

A judge evaluating the marching execution should make comments regarding carriage (posture) when standing still and when moving, uniformity of foot placement, synchronization, uniformity of body movements, pivots, turns, facings, step-offs, halts, mark time, manipulation of instruments and equipment, recovery from error, ranks, files, arcs, set arrival, and intervals. The marching judge also addresses the drill design by commenting on the compatibility of the band's marching style

The early-morning sun creates an interesting additional effect to this opening formation of a contest routine. A judge will take note of how seamlessly the band transitions between formations.

to the drill; the difficulty, frequency, and rigor of movement; continuity and flow; visual reinforcement of the music; effective use of the auxiliary units (dance and drill teams and color guard); and the appearance of the uniforms.

Each judge assigns a score that is either used in its raw form or converted to a number representing how the judge has ranked the group in comparison to the others. (The conversion is highest score first, lowest score last.) The rank scores are then added across the judging panel in order to either total or average all of the judges' rankings. The band with the lowest rank total or average is declared the competition winner.

The weight of importance of each attribute of judging may vary from one contest to another and depend on age classification or levels of ability. It must be understood that a certain amount of a judge's perceptions are subjective rather than objective. Each judge presents scores that reflect his or her personal likes and dislikes.

Performers take a risk when subjecting their work to the opinions of others. You should understand that the ultimate goal of a competition is not winning; it's creating the best possible overall performance. Success should be measured by the band's progress, and winning should be taken as recognition of a performance well done. If another band is recognized over yours, it is best to applaud it. It will always feel great when you know you have done your very best.

# CHAPTER
## 5

# Beyond High School

Extending your involvement in marching band activities outside of high school can include being a member of a drum and bugle corps organization, such as those affiliated with Drum Corps International (DCI). These groups consist of drums, brass, and color guards. They begin rehearsals in late winter and early spring for performances throughout the summer months.

Snare drum carriage has evolved from an over-the-shoulder sling with the drum on the side of the leg to a double-shoulder hanger attached to the drum for frontal carriage. The hanger can be adjusted to fit the height of the drum to the performer.

Each of these organizations is allowed to have up to 128 members composed of fourteen- to twenty-one-year-old performers. The groups also rehearse while on tour. They travel all over the United States to compete against other groups. The tour season ends with the Drum Corps International World Championships, held in August, just in time for the performers to return to their high schools or colleges.

Those who choose not to participate with DCI can attend summer band camps. Although these camps are not specific to marching bands, they are designed to further a student's specific instrumental music,

The Notre Dame snare drum section leads the Irish Band out of the stadium tunnel and onto the field for a pregame show.

conducting, music theory, composition, and jazz skills. Some camps specifically target those who are, or wish to become, drum majors. Specialty training is provided in conducting technique, motivating peers, and being a team leader. Many students attend several camps each summer, with a different focus at each camp.

Colleges and universities prefer to admit high school students who have participated in extracurricular activities and demonstrated academic success and leadership. Marching bands provide an excellent

The Allen High School "Eagle Escadrille" from Allen, Texas, performs in the 117th Rose Parade in Pasadena, California. The band has more than 400 members.

way for students to do this. Music programs at the college level are also willing to provide scholarships to students who will participate in the band programs. Music education scholarships are available for those who choose to make music education their major field of study. In some cases, there are even full-tuition scholarships that are granted to talented music majors. Announcements of scholarships can be found on college Web sites and in music education journals across the country.

Many high school band members go on to music careers. Some become marching band instructors. Others become composers and conductors. Still others become professional musicians, either in classical or theatrical orchestras or in popular music. Many pop and jazz musicians got their start in school band programs. Even for those band members who don't pursue careers in music, marching band is a rewarding, fun experience. It teaches important life lessons, such as teamwork, dedication, and discipline, and it provides the basis for many lifelong friendships.

# GLOSSARY

**alma mater**  The anthem or school song of a high school, college, or university.

**carriage**  The manner of holding and carrying one's head and body; posture or bearing.

**cheer blaster**  A short musical statement designed to create spirit and support for the spectators and participants in an athletic event.

**chorale**  A musical composition based on a hymn.

**color guard**  An auxiliary unit that performs using flags, rifles, and sabers as props.

**composition**  An original work of music written for specific instrumentation and/or voicings.

**curvilinear**  In marching bands, a drill design based on forms of bounded, continuous curves and lines.

**drum cadence**  A composition for the percussion section of the band, most commonly used in street parades between the selections by the full band.

**drum major**  One who leads a marching band, usually a student member of the band.

**etude**  A piece of music designed to develop a particular point of performance technique.

**file**  In marching band, a line of members in front-to-back alignment.

**front**  In marching band, a line of members in left-to-right (side-by-side) alignment.

**melody**  A rhythmic succession of single tones organized as an aesthetic whole.

**mirror conducting**  In marching band, the matching of music conducting by two or more drum majors.

**performance memory**  The ability to perform written music from memory.

**phasing**  In marching band, the loss of unified rhythmical accuracy between the performers because of the distance between performers.

**quin-tom**  A set of five different-size drums, usually mounted to a frame suitable for carrying the drums while marching.

**rendition**  An interpretation and performance of a musical score or dramatic piece.

**scale**  A progression of music notes in a specific ascending and descending order.

**set**  A picture or formation in a drill design and the relative placement on the field.

**solo**  A musical composition for a single voice or instrument with or without accompaniment; the featured part of a concerto or similar work.

**summer band**  Marching band and auxiliary rehearsals usually during a school's summer vacation period.

**synchronization**  The simultaneous occurrence of similar or related events; the occurrence of an event in time to a musical rhythm; unison.

**tone**  The characteristic quality or timbre of a particular instrument or voice.

# For More Information

Bands of America
39 W. Jackson Place, Suite 150
Indianapolis, IN 46225
(800) 848-BAND (2263)
Web site: http://www.bands.org

Drum Corps International
470 South Imen Drive
Addison, IL 60101
(630) 628-7888
Web site: http://www.dci.org

## Web Sites

Due to the changing nature of Internet links, the Rosen Publishing
Group, Inc., has developed an online list of Web sites related to the
subject of this book. This site is updated regularly. Please use this link
to access the list:

http://www.rosenlinks.com/team/maba

# For Further Reading

Fyffe, Daniel. *Indoor Percussion Ensembles and Drum Corps.* New York, NY: Rosen Publishing Group, 1997.

Garty, Judy. *Techniques of Marching Bands.* Philadelphia, PA: Mason Crest Publishers, 2003.

Hurd, Michael. *Soldiers' Songs and Marches.* New York, NY: H. Z. Walck, 1966.

Lillegard, Dee. *Brass: An Introduction to Musical Instruments.* Chicago, IL: Children's Press, 1988.

Markham, Lynne. *The Closing March.* London, England: Mammoth, 1997.

Porterfield, Jason. *Band Front: Color Guard, Band Majors, and Majorettes.* New York, NY: Rosen Publishing Group, 1997.

Sousa, John Philip. *Marching Along.* Boston, MA: Hale, Cushman and Flint, 1928.

Turner, Gordon, and Alwyn Turner. *The History of British Military Bands.* 3 vols. Vol. 1: *Cavalry & Corps.* Kent, England: Spellmount, 1994.

Weil, Ann. *John Philip Sousa: Marching Boy.* Indianapolis, IN: Bobbs-Merrill, 1959.

Wells, James R. *The Marching Band in Contemporary Music Education.* New York, NY: Interland Publishing, 1976.

# Bibliography

Apel, Willi. *The Harvard Dictionary of Music.* Cambridge, MA: Harvard University Press, 1974.

Holston, Kim R. *The Marching Band Handbook.* 2nd ed. Jefferson, NC: McFarland & Company, 1994.

Lee, William F. *Music Theory Dictionary: The Language of the Mechanics of Music.* New York, NY: Charles Hansen Educational Music and Books, 1966.

RBC Music. *Pocket Music Dictionary.* Milwaukee, WI: Hal Leonard Publishing, 1993.

Robinson, William C. *The Complete School Band Program.* West Nyack, NY: Parker Publishing Company, Inc., 1975.

*Microsoft Encarta Online Encyclopedia.* "Sousa, John Philip." 2005. Retrieved October 1, 2005 (http://encarta.msn.com/encyclopedia_761554554/Sousa_John_Philip.html).

# Index

## About the Author

Frank Coachman assumed the duties of deputy director for the Texas Music Educators Association (TMEA) in July 1999. For the previous twenty-two years, Coachman served the music education profession in the Killeen Independent School District. For eighteen of those years, he served as director of bands for C. E. Ellison High School. Coachman was president of TMEA, and was state band vice-president from 1990 to 1992, region band chair from 1983 to 1990, and region jazz chair from 1981 to 1984. He attended Texas Tech University and graduated from McMurry University with a B.F.A. in music education. In 2002, Coachman was named Honorary Life Member of the Texas Music Adjudicators Association. He is much in demand as a conductor, clinician, adjudicator, composer-arranger, and music education curriculum consultant.

Series Consultant: Susan Epstein

## Photo Credits

Cover, pp. 44, 49 Mark Hansen; title page © Phil Schermeister/Corbis; pp. 5, 26 Ron Eichstedt, Jr.; p. 7 © David Young-Wolff/Photo Edit; p. 8 © Brian Bahr/Getty Images; p. 9 © Bryan Rinnert/ZUMA/Corbis; p. 10 © Corbis; p. 11 Frank Coachman; pp. 13, 24, 27, 30, 34, 38, 42 Ayala High School Band and Color Guard, Chino Hills, CA., Mark Stone, Director; pp. 13, 27, 30, 34 photos by Jose A. Fernandez; p. 15 © William Thomas Cain/ Getty Images; p. 17 Bateman Photography; p. 18 © David R. Frazier Photolibrary, Inc./ Alamy; p. 19 © James Shaffer/Photo Edit; p. 21 © Ariel Skelley/Corbis; p. 23 © Tom & Dee Ann McCarthy/Corbis; p. 28 © VStock/Alamy; p. 32 Bob Bivens Photography; p. 35 © Smiley N. Pool/Dallas Morning News/Corbis; p. 40 © Jason Braverman/epa/Corbis; p. 41 © Donald Miralle/Getty Images; p. 46 © Tom Carter/Photo Edit; p. 48 Ron Walloch; p. 51 Sanger High School, Sanger, TX; p. 53 © Gary Conner/Photo Edit; p. 54 © Dennis MacDonald/Alamy; p. 55 © Icon SMI/Corbis; p. 56 © Lucas Jackson/Reuters/Corbis.

Designer: Gene Mollica; Editor: Wayne Anderson; Photo Researcher: Marty Levick